TABLE OF CONTENTS

Introduction

You know, you have seen books and movies, how people fall in love and get married and live happily ever after? Right? Well, what if I told you the exact opposite? Would you still be sitting there watching? Reading? Would you still be interested in what is going on? Or would you just close the book up and or the movie and eject it? Well, let's get started, shall we?

My name is Delilah Jane Holloway. We live in the hills of Kentucky. My dad works at the coal mines down in our small town called browns. It's just a small town. No Biggy. Our time period is around 1940. Its winter times. My Mother disappeared after my little sister was born. It's sad really. I stay home cook breakfast, lunch and dinner. Clean, do dishes and laundry. While most kids my age attend school. DO homework and so much more. I have never been to school. When dad comes home that is when I go to the basement.

He won't allow me to go outside. It's odd really. But, its life….

Chapter one

whispers

Browns Kentucky

Winter 1970

My name is Jack Courtright. I am almost ten years old. My mom and I Moved into my grandpa's house, shortly after my parent's divorce. I haven't seen my dad in years. God knows where he is.

But this story isn't about him. See that girl in the picture frame, on my grandpa's wall? It's a silver picture frame. A family portrait. We were always told it was a family friend. But really, it was my mother's older sister we never knew about. This is her story on how we found out she existed.

It's funny how the people you love the most contact you after they had passed. It's funny how they try so hard to get your attention in your life. And you're so busy. You never get it?

Funny, how life goes sometimes like that. We were unloading our station wagon outside and mom was tired, I could tell. I told her to get some blankets and go lay down while I unpacked the car.

We finally got unpacked, I was moving boxes in, and went upstairs. Too look to find a room for me. I opened the doorknob. There were white walls, and wooden bases and cobwebs in the windows, I carried my stuff in. then later we brought the furniture and stuff in from the uhall van outside. It was slowly looking like our old home in New York. But, when your broke and out of money and half no place to go. Suddenly home seems like a nice word know matter where you've landed. It took some time, but we finally got moved in after a month or so being there.

Chapter one

Somewhere in Kentucky

Spring

1970 Delilah's POV

I remember this day, very vividly. It was mid-summer, almost may. My sister was coming. It was just me and my mom in the house. My dad was at work in the coal mine. He worked long hours. My dad was never around hardly because of it. I was close to my mom. She had been having labour pains, the last couple of hours. I was probably about ten years old.

"Lilly belle. I need you to do me a favour." Momma said, holding her belly with pain covering it up so I couldn't see her in pain.

"What's the matter momma?" I asked her to look at her confused.

"Can, you run next door and ask Mrs. Johnson, to come over tell her the baby is coming and I need some help." She said to me falling to the floor screaming in pain.

"Okay momma, I will go get her." I said running out the door. I ran across to next door to see if Mrs. Johnson was home.

You could hear me shouting for Mrs Johnson, two miles down the road. I found her outside in her garden she jumped up startle.

"What's the matter Delilah?" She asked me curiously.

"Momma said she needs your help the baby is coming, and daddy isn't home." I said to her. She got up from her knees from planting flowers and veggies in her garden, and we both ran next door.

Mrs. Johnson called the hospital, and daddy, to tell him to come home. The baby was coming. They took momma to the hospital, but I stayed behind, with Mrs Johnson, so momma could have my baby sister.

Daddy came home that night, without momma. He had tears in his eyes. Mrs. Johnson came over and told me goodbye and went home.

"Dad, are you okay?" I asked him curiously.

He threw his hat, on the table, and picked up a cigar.

"I will be." He said lighting his cigar and sitting down on the table.

"You look angry dad, is something wrong?" I asked her.

"I guess there is no easy way to say this Lilly belle." He said to me squatting down on my level. "We have a new member of the family. Jane Elizabeth Holloway. Eight pounds nine ounces and 17 inches long." He said to me proudly.

"That's good. I can't wait to see my new sister. Is mom okay?" I asked him as a tear fell down his cheek.

"Baby, she didn't make it." He said with complete sadness.

I got a deathly ghostly look on my face. Tears fell down my cheek and I ran out the door and ran out to mine and moms spot, over by the pond. We used to have picnics in our back yard. We lived out in the country. I cried and cried, then suddenly, I seen Bailey, chosen after a duck, and I tried to get him out of the water. The next thing I know, I hear my dad scream my name a bunch of times.

"I can't lose you too." My dad said crying holding my lifeless body in his arms.

"Hold on baby!" Daddy cried as I laid in his arms clinging for dear life, he tried and tried to save me yelling help. But death knows no age, nor limits.

Present time

Jack Holloways Point of view

You know, life has a way at working things out. My name is Jack David Holloway. I just turned 12 a few days ago. Everything was fine, for once mom and dad wasn't fighting or each, others, throats. But I knew something was up. After all my friends left. My parents sat me down in the living room.

"Okay, lay it on me." I said to them.

"Lay what on who?" Mom said to me.

"Somethings got to give. You two aren't fighting. What's going on?" I asked them questionable.

"We decided, that we need to move on with out each other honey. Were just unhappy fighting all the time. It's not good for either of us, or you as well." Mom said walking over to me and sitting down by me on the sofa.

"Doesn't surprise me." I said throwing my hands up in the air. "Are we moving are you getting a divorce?" I asked them.

"Yes, you and I are moving to the house out in the country on the south side of Kentucky, far away from here." She said to me looking down at her shoes.

"Great." I said to her, looking at dad, I got up, and stormed down the hallway and slammed the door shut. "This suck." I said as I slammed it hard and pictures fell on the floor.

I had gone upstairs to my bedroom to get away from the obvious people just made me mad today I didn't want to go anywhere or do anything except be miserable for a while. And I had fell sleep on my bed my mom came in and put covers on me about two or three hours later, a grown dark outside. The next day Mom and I had packed up everything at our old house and move to our new house in Kentucky.

Janes Point of View

I was picking up the living room and putting boxes away when Jack was in his room sleeping. I was hanging pictures up of Jack and I throughout the house. Pictures of us growing up. Then, I opened the door, and inside was a doll. My baby doll I had as a baby. She had aged and next to her on the floor was a picture of a young lady, and a me when I was about a year old. I squinted my eyes. I couldn't figure her out I never seen her before. I grabbed the blanket out of the closet, and I through the doll halfway across the room because, I was so mad at my soon to be ex hubby. For leaving Jack and me.

Then all of a sudden I was getting ready to turn around, and the next thing I know the doll fly's back and smacks my face I was so angry and so mad I shrieked because I was scared at the same time I didn't know what was going on and all happened so fast and check came running down the whole way to check on me we were trying to say get the doll away from my face and Jack grabbed it off of my hand and threw it across the room and stepped on its head and it finally died.

I set up with blood all over my face in a panic mode trying to figure out exactly what just happened that's the kind of stuff that happens in movies and you read about it, but does it happen? I mean for real was I hallucinating or you scream at the top of my voice through the door I have for with blood all over my face in a panic mode trying to figure out exactly what just happened that's the kind of stuff that happens in movies and you read about it but does it actually happened? I mean for real was I hallucinating?

Jackie running down the hallway to check on me to make sure I was OK he was in shock that there was blood all over my face and there was a doll that was laying there lifeless on the floor with its eyes staring up at us as it shimmered in the dark.

"What the hell happened? "Jack had asked me shockingly looking at the doll and then looking at me.

"How do you watch your mouth? "I sent catching my breath as I was in a panic. "You wouldn't believe me if I told you! "I had said getting myself up off the floor and looking for something to clean up with as I went to the bathroom and jack had follow me.

I grabbed a washcloth and begin the cleanup but that was on my face and there was not much scarring left just a few skirts and bruises, but it was gonna leave a mark and how was I going to explain this one is someone had asked. And I got attacked by any Chan grabbed a washcloth and begin the cleanup but that was on my face and there was not much scarring left just a few skirts and bruises but it

"Mom who is the older girl?" he asked me. "isn't that you as the baby? "he asked concerned like.

"I think so." I had said taking a second glance. I never seen the woman before in my life she lives far too young to be having a baby in her arms was that my mother. I never seen a picture before of her she died when I was young. When she gave birth to me, she did not make it. She bled out before the doctors could safe her. or so I was told. And I guess there's only one person that could tell me who this woman was. that was aunt Ruth. I walked downstairs and went to the kitchen and phoned and it was in the middle of the daytime Surely, she was up.

"Hello?" Aunt Ruth said on the other end of the phone.

"Hi Aunt Ruth, its Jane." I said to her standing sitting down on the kitchen chair.

"Hi Jane, how are you and Jack doing everything okay?" She asked curiously.

"Well, kind of. Jack found a photo of me with a young lady, and I have never seen or heard about her. Do you think you can come over and look at it to see who she is?" I asked her curiously.

"Sure, I would be happy to. This afternoon okay? She asked me.

"Yes, the sooner the better." I replied to her.

"Okay I will come over after lunch." She said to me.

" I have a few things for you and Jack anyway." She said to me seriously.

"Aw, well it be great to catch up." I said to her.

"Yep, see you then honey, I got to finish my sewing projects." She said to me talking fast.

"Okay Have a good morning." I said to her hanging up the phone as I turned around and jack was standing behind me.

"What did she say?" he asked.

"She's going to come over this afternoon to look at it." I smiled.

"mom, what are you going to tell Aunt Ruth about your face?" He asked me concerned.

"Good, point." I said to him. "Ran in to a door." I said to him as he laughed and went back to his room

Chapter two ruths wings

It had been a long hard summer; it's been hard on Jack. He had been away from everything he's ever known. But the thing is it grew us closer. I needed him as much as he needed me. There was a knock on the door and been Aunt Ruth. she come over to see who the girl was in the picture. But we really didn't know what we were getting ourselves into that day. the Screen door was wide open so you could see who is standing on the porch and Jane had a long purple dress on. She always had the finest of the finest.

"Hello anyone home? "Aunt Jane had asked.

"we're in here" I shouted from the kitchen.

Jack and I we're at the kitchen table. We were going through old photos that we had found in the basement. Jack found a trunk, over by the window. It looked like you had never been gone through before untouched for years it was sitting over by the window. Aunt Ruth looked scared she had looked like she had seen a ghost.

"Hi aunt Ruth how are you! "Jack said giving her a hug.

"Where did you get that trunk!! "She said freaking out.

"We found it in the basement. Is everything ok?" I asked Aunt Ruth.

"You need to put it back." She said getting upset.

"It got old photos in it from our family." Jack said walking back over towards the table. She began to get ghostly white; Aunt Ruth didn't look so good.

"Are, you sure you're okay?" I asked.

"Darling, some things are not to be meddled with. What have you saw so far?" she asked cautiously.

One moment it went from a family gathering to an interrogation.

"Just old pictures of that girl, Jack saw." I said to her.

"Put the trunk back where you found it. You need to get out of this house now." Aunt Ruthie said picking up the old pictures and putting them back in the trunk. Jack and I looked at her confused. We had no idea what she was talking about.

"I'll find you a nice place in town for you and Lil Jack. In town. You shouldn't have come here in the first

place. It's too dangerous." She began to explain.

"What do you mean?" I asked.

"Come to my house. Don't bring any pictures with you, I'll explain everything." Aunt Ruth began to leave and then suddenly, we heard a little girl's laughter. Jacks face got ghostly white and split out the front door, I had never seen him leave so fast before in my life.

"Aunt Ruthie, do you want to play with me?" The little girl said as the pots and pans began to shake on the wall.

Aunt Ruth came over and grabbed my hand and out the door we went.

The door slammed shut after we left.

We went down to aunt ruthie's house, I had never seen anything like that house before in my life. It was defiantly one for the books.

We started to get in the car, but when aunt ruthie's got in the car, the doors locked, she tried to get out of the car, and knocked on the window screaming for help as loud as she could we were screaming help as well. Then suddenly, the car exploded. Out of nowhere.

I covered Jacks eyes as Aunt Ruthie burnt to a crisp inside the car.

We turned our heads. I called the ambulance and the cops, and they came and picked up the car, and aunt Ruth what was left.

I told them the car exploded, due to heat conditions. If I would have told them my house was haunted, my son would be going back to his father and I would be put in the house with white coats. They would think I am crazy.

I look up after the police and everyone had been gone and saw this image of a young girl standing outside my window, and I saw her red eyes and then vanished.

Chapter three

Teacups and baby dolls

After Aunt Ruth's, funeral we began to dig for answers. We were scared out of our minds and didn't know what to do. You know that moment when you think the worst was over? As if loosing Ruth wasn't enough. It had just begun to get worse. I don't know how much we can take before we lose our minds. We were lying in bed in the middle of the night. Jack couldn't sleep by himself he was to be scared. Truth be told. I was to. Suddenly about three am. The pictures began to raddle on the walls the shadow of their eyes grew red, and the door was open, but it slammed shut, and began to glow a slightly orange glow, shimmering through the cracks. We began to get scared; Jack was in tears.

"mom!" He shrieked   out loud as he buried his head in my arms. We laid there helplessly, as this shadow of a girl stood before her bed.

"What do you want?" I asked her. She didn't say anything. But pointed out towards the shed, and the pond area. An, simply vanished.

the next morning

Jack had woken up the next morning and was playing video games with a buddy he had made next door. His name was Ethan. Seemed like a nice young man. But still it was nice to see jack at a chance of normalcy and making friends. For that reason, we would have to solve this thing. At least for my son's sake.

I fixed something to eat and went and went outside to work in the garden for a while. I peeked inside and a few more kids came over which was amazing. I was so proud of him for making a big bunch of friends. Making even one at his age is hard.

I turned around and saw the shed that the young woman was pointing at.

I walked over towards the shed and saw baby dolls that had one eye sticking out, and pieces of parts missing I thought it was kind of morbid. But I went inside any way.

There was a living room, in the front part of the shed that had pictures of my mother and father and this young girl that was jacks age. About ten or twelve. I had never seen her before in my life or even herd of her before. Is it possible that she is still alive today? And if so where is she. Without aunt Ruth, here to help how could we find out?

FOR REAL! I couldn't wait for those children to leave so I could tell Jack about the shed. There was a bathroom and a small kitchenet and looked like a bedroom that was boarded shut. I decided not to go in because, I was too scared at the point time. So, I walked back out of the shed and locked it. And put the key in my po

Chapter four

Letter box

I had gone upstairs to the attic, because I wanted to see what else I could find. While the boys played video games downstairs. I was really interested and finding at least something to prove she existed. Sure, we had all these photos, and all these dolls and even a room but all that means nothing. She had to have some form of identification or government information.

I looked around, and found an old trunk over by the window, I was throwing stuff everywhere and didn't care at the time being. I looked at the trunk and the old cabinet on the left-hand side. I wanted to go through the cabinet after the trunk. I opened the old trunk and found a bunch of things. I found baby doll clothes hats and bonnets, and a stack of letters. They had Delilah S Halloway written all over them from mom and dad on them. They had to put her in an institution for young girls. Then I put the letters over to the side and found a bunch of pictures, in the cabinet.

"By Jack see you Saturday!" One by stated as I heard them yell out the window. I walked over towards the window and watched them leave.

I grabbed the letters and the pictures and went downstairs to be with Jack. Finally!

"Jack?" I asked questionably.

"Hey mom." He said coming in and sitting down at the table to eat some pizza he had sweet tea to drink.

"I found a room outside in the shed, and some old letters and pictures. Would you like to see the room?" I asked him curiously.

"Sure." He said slugging some more pizza down.

We went outside, and I opened the door with the key, and we looked inside. There was nothing but mowers and garden tools there.

"Where's the room?" Jack asked curiously.

"No! it was right here, I saw it!" I shouted looking all over everywhere I found a teddy bear with missing eyes and the doll I found was sitting over by the window was on the lawn mower.

"It's okay mom. "Jack said. "Let's go look at the letters and pictures." Jack said to me.

We walked out of the shed, and as soon as we walked out the door slammed shut and it started to poor down rain.

We ran inside the house as we got weirded out by the rain. We walked in the kitchen and sat down at the kitchen table. We started reading the letters out loud to one another.

We found out that aunt Ruth lied about the drowning when she was a little girl. We found out in a letter that dad kept her up in the attic and in the shed because, was mentally disturbed and wanted to hurt people or animals. I wonder what made her that way?

There must be a reason, or a purpose, for it. I mean you just don't get that way over night, right?

Chapter five

Delilah's pov

Dear diary,

Did you ever wonder why the grass is green and the sky is blue? I mean they go hand in hand together, but did you ever wonder why they were that precise color? Was it for a purpose or for a reason? Just like me being tortured and being forced to stay inside all because my dad didn't want to have children?

I mean, you would think a person would want that. After finding their true love, but honestly, after being kept inside for all these years your skin starts to change color, your eyes are accepted to sunlight, your brain is gone and there's nothing left but a frail monster, to society.

So, my question to you is dear reader of this dreadful story. Are you glad you can exist? Because, I would love to be noticed.

Just one bone chilling time. Did, I capture your soul and your spirit? Did, I haunt you till the day in your dreams, and you can toss and turn about? In all honesty! It was just a story in a book! But I hope it stuck in the back of your brain!

Sincerely

We are the Halloway!

Until next time!

Chapter six

You know, this never crossed my mind in to how I would die, or even if I would die. But everyone has their time. I never even thought my older dead sibling would do it. In a million years. But it was the way it was transcribed.

I was home by myself Jack as in bed asleep. I always told him if something like this would to happen, it would be Delilah. She had been coming into my room at night just watching us sleep. Jack wouldn't sleep by himself. So, he slept, with me.

We kept the closet light on like that would help. We put holy water on the windows and in the doors where she would come. But even that didn't help.

It was like nothing we did would drive her away. We were too proud to move.

I dimmed the lights to take a bath. I kept the door slightly open, I stood there for a second hesitant to get in. But I was dying for a bubble bath. After finding that stuff. I turned on the water and got in, I was in for a good hour and the water started to get deathly cold, and then the temperature of the water and the room suddenly changed, and the water started to drain down the tub really fast, and I know this is crazy, but I tried and tried to get out of the tub. But it sucked my spirit down the drain and all I heard was a little girl giggle like a school child. She turned into a snake head, that popped out of the bathtub, and took me down the drain.

"I told you, you would play with me." She skipped about. Ring around the Rosie, pocket full of posies. Ashes, ashes baby jane goes down." She laughed her head off as I heard jack scream no at the top of his lungs.

"momma! Please no!" he squealed he cried and cried at my lifeless body cringing for dear life, he got up and called 911 but by the time they got to our house out in the country. It was too late. I had been gone.

The workers took Jack to his dad's house. I often worry about Jack. But I know he is a strong young man. More of me inside him. I guess we all have hauntings from our past that haunt us. It's just up to us if we let them decide if we go or not.

I guess, I couldn't take it no longer and that's why I let Delilah take me like I did. I could have fought harder. I could have held on longer. But there is only so much pain one can endure. Sometimes it gets the best of us.

<u>Note from author!</u>

hi everyone, this is author Lizabeth mars! I just want to tell everyone thank you so much for purchasing and reading my books! Especially this series! Because, when I was younger, I use to be so terrified of watching scary movies no matter how scary it was I would go in the other room! LOL never in my wildest dreams I would think I would be writing short scary stories! But wicked lil dreamz is a new short story scary books for young adults and adults of all ages who like to get scared! Anyways thanks again!

Made in the USA
Columbia, SC
09 January 2020